© SostegnO 2.0 Editori
1° Edizione settembre 2022

www.sostegno20.it
info@sostegno20.it

Tutti i diritti riservati. Vietata la riproduzione con qualsiasi mezzo effettuata, se non previa autorizzazione dell'Editore. È consentita la fotocopiatura delle schede operative a esclusivo uso didattico.

SOSTEGNO 2.0

INDICE

About me.. pag.4
Greetings... pag.6
Numbers.. pag.8
Colors... pag.14
Days of the week...................................... pag.29
Month of the year..................................... pag.34
The four seasons...................................... pag.37
School objects... pag.51
Clothes... pag.56
Weather.. pag.60
Food and drink.. pag.62
Toys... pag.66
Body parts.. pag.71
Feels.. pag.75
Means of transport.................................. pag.77
Family members..................................... pag.80
Daily routine... Pag.83

Animals.. pag.85
Opposites... pag.91
Adjectives.. pag.94
What time is it? pag.98
I can.. pag.106
Have got... pag.113
Verb to be.. pag.117
There is/there are............................... pag.119
Prepositions of place.......................... pag.121
Possessive pronous.............................. pag.124
Some-any.. pag.130
Clil.. pag.133
Activty book.. pag.137

English

My name is ....
My teacher is ....
My school is ....

About Me

My school is called: _____

I am in grade: _____

My teacher's name is: _____

My favourite subject is: _____

Draw yourself

Colors how you got to school today:

   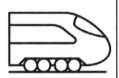

GREETINGS

I SALUTI

NUMBERS

I NUMERI

Numbers

Write the numbers

one   four   three   ten   eight   zero
seven   nine   five   two   six

0   1   2   3

----   ----   ----   ----

4   5   6

----   ----   ----

7   8   9   10

----   ----   ----   ---

Number Pyramid

Cut out and paste the numbers on to the matching written numbers

eleven

twelve   thirteen

fourteen   fifteen   sixteen

seventeen   eighteen   nineteen   twenty

18   14   12   20   17

11   16   15   13   19

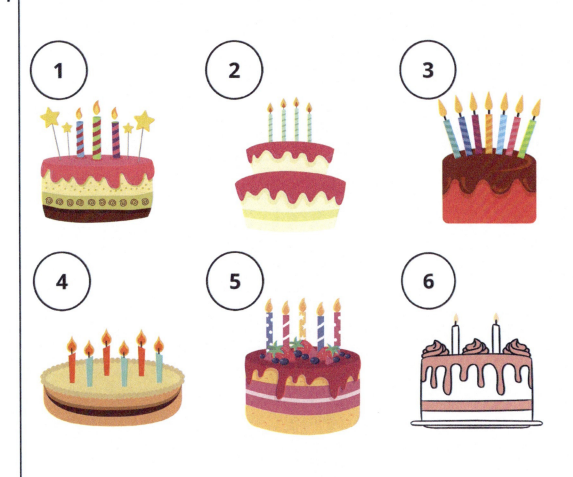

- María is five years old.   CAKE: _____
- Luke is two years old.   CAKE: _____
- Mark is seven years old.   CAKE: _____
- Anna is three years old.   CAKE: _____
- Rob is six years old.   CAKE: _____
- Vic is four years old.   CAKE: _____

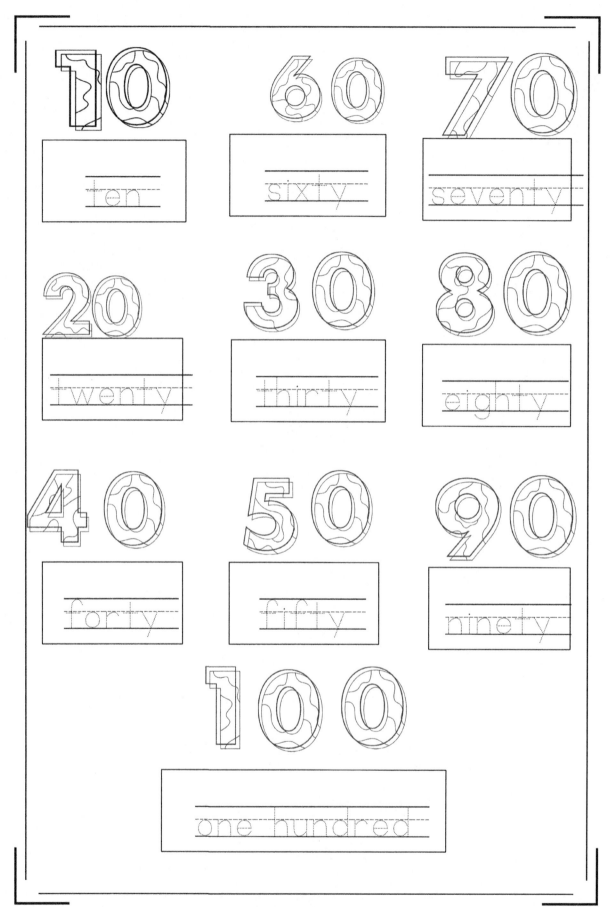

Write the correct answers in the space provided.

before

___ 5

___ 44

___ 21

___ 56

___ 13

between

78 ___ 80

2 ___ 4

34 ___ 36

67 ___ 69

90 ___ 92

after

58 ___

89 ___

45 ___

77 ___

17 ___

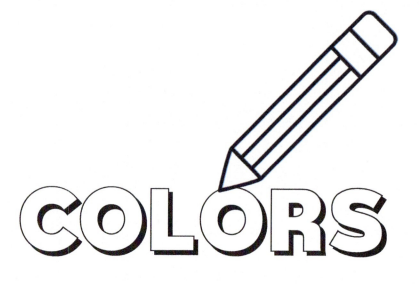

COLORS

I COLORI

Color the clouds

Colors Memotest

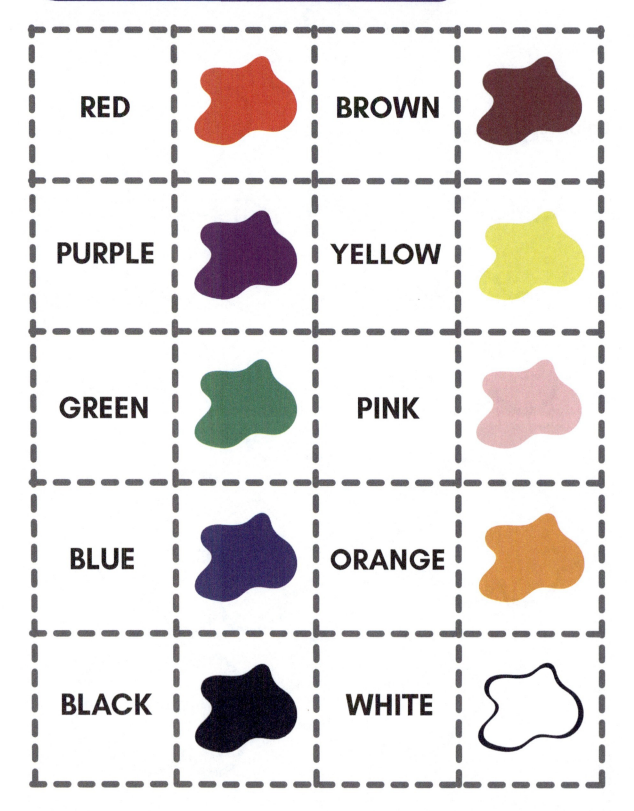

I like color

RED!

Color all the things that are red

Build the word.

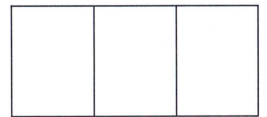

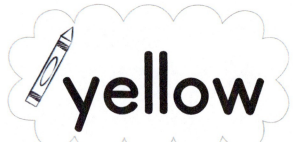

Color all the things that are yellow

yellow _____

Build the word.

Color all the things that are green.

green

Build the word.

I like color PINK!

pink

Color all the things that are pink.

pink

Build the word.

I like color PURPLE!

purple

Color all the things that are purple.

purple _____

Build the word.

I like color ORANGE!

orange

Color all the things that are orange.

orange _____

Build the word.

I like color BLUE!

blue

Color all the things that are blue.

blue _____

Build the word.

I like color BLACK!

black

Color all the things that are black.

black _____

Build the word.

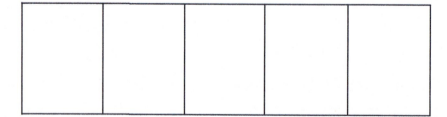

 I like color BROWN!

 brown

Color all the things that are brown.

brown _____

Build the word.

 I like color GREY!  grey

Color all the things that are grey.

grey _____

Build the word.

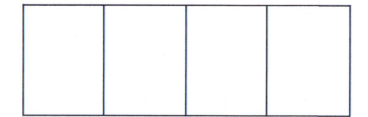

 I like color WHITE!

white

Circle all the things that are white.

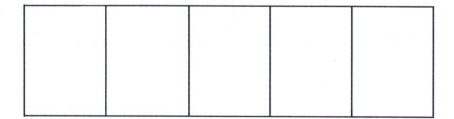
white

Build the word.

Dog Color by Number

Use the key at the bottom of the page to color the picture.

1. white   2. red   3. brown   4. green   5. blue   6. grey

DAYS OF THE WEEK

I GIORNI DELLA SETTIMANA

Days of the Week

Write the correct answers in the space provided.

Yesterday	Today	Tomorrow
_____	Wednesday	_____
_____	Friday	_____
_____	Tuesday	_____
_____	Sunday	_____
_____	Thursday	_____

DAYS OF THE WEEK

Fill in the blanks for the days of the week:

Days of the week

Find the days of the week

S	A	T	U	R	D	A	Y	D	O	H
J	O	H	P	F	R	I	D	A	Y	L
M	A	U	T	H	T	A	R	I	N	S
N	I	R	M	S	U	N	D	A	Y	K
C	K	S	O	L	E	T	V	I	A	G
W	E	D	N	E	S	D	A	Y	Y	R
M	A	A	D	A	D	A	Y	A	Y	T
L	I	Y	A	N	A	O	U	P	S	D
L	O	M	Y	M	Y	T	U	S	D	F

Days of the Week

✂ Cut along the dotted lines. Glue the days of the week in the correct order into your scrapbook.

Saturday

Monday

Wednesday

Friday

Sunday

Tuesday

Thursday

MONTHS OF THE YEAR

I MESI DELL'ANNO

Months of the Year

Write the correct answers in the space provided.

last month	this month	next month
_____	November	_____
_____	March	_____
_____	July	_____
_____	September	_____
_____	January	_____

Months of the Year

✂ Cut along the dotted lines. Glue the months of the year in the correct order into your scrapbook.

March

June

April

December

September

November

January

October

July

February

May

August

THE FOUR SEASON

LE QUATTRO STAGIONI

The Four Season

Color the pictures and draw a line to match the pictures to the season.

   Winter

   Spring

   Summer

   Autumn

Color and Find Season

Directions: Color the pictures. Cut and paste the pictures into the correct box.

Winter	Spring
Summer	Autumn

✂ -

OUR FAVORITE SEASON

Tally your class's favorite season and record in the graph:

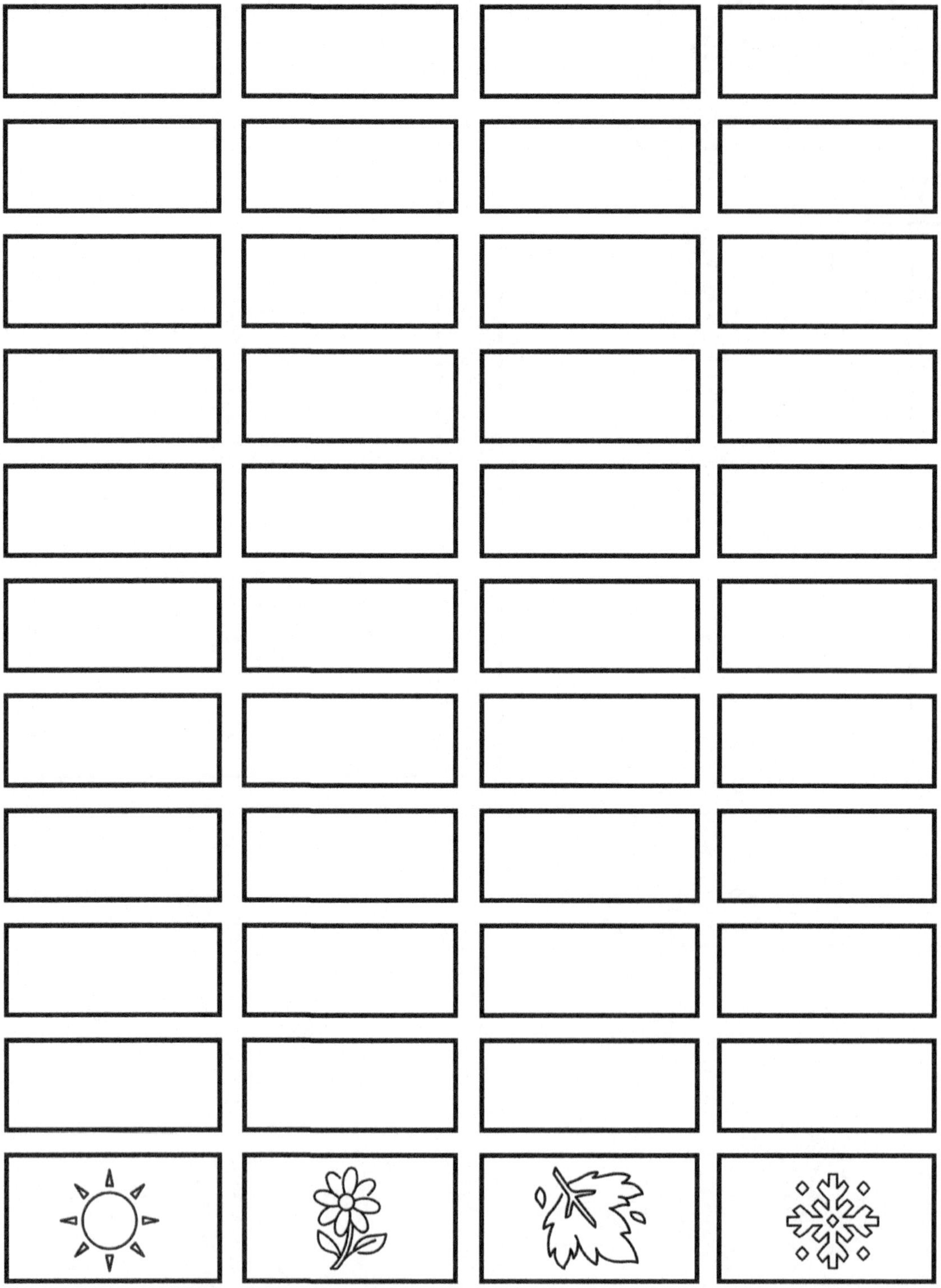

SEASONS

Find-a-word

A	U	T	U	M	N	K	O	N	U	S
W	A	R	R	E	H	T	A	E	W	P
I	E	A	R	T	H	N	G	A	H	R
N	T	R	E	V	O	L	V	E	U	I
T	S	A	Z	O	I	E	G	R	R	N
E	N	T	H	R	E	E	T	E	C	G
R	O	L	Y	A	G	E	R	M	H	N
R	S	E	N	R	D	A	E	M	N	D
I	A	H	F	O	U	R	N	U	A	E
R	E	X	L	A	V	I	T	S	E	F
S	S	W	A	R	M	E	S	T	C	O

- SEASON
- WEATHER
- YEAR
- FOUR
- SUMMER
- AUTUMN
- WINTE
- SUMMER
- SPRING
- EARH
- REOLVE
- SUN
- THREE
- WARMEST

41

SPRING

Answer the following prompts about spring.

Spring makes me feel...

" In spring I see... "

In spring I like to...

Draw a spring picture

SUMMER

Answer the following prompts about summer

AUTUMN

Answer the following prompts about spring.

- autumn makes me feel...
- In autumn I see...
- In autumn I like to...
- Draw a sautumn picture

WINTER

Answer the following prompts about winter

winter makes me feel...

" In winter I see... "

In winter like to...

Draw a winter

Days of the Week

Cut around the days of the week and place them in order.

	Tuesday
	Thursday
	Sunday
	Monday
	Saturday
	Wednesday
	Friday

Months of the Year

Cut around the months of the year and place them in order.

	March
	June
	September
	April
	November
	February
	August
	July
	January
	December
	October
	May

Seasons of the Year

Cut round each season and place in order from the start of the year

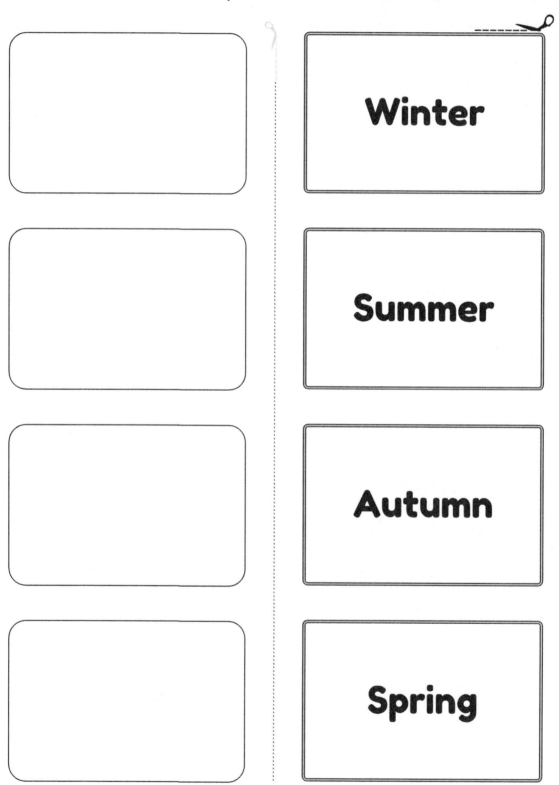

48

Seasons of the Year

Cut round each picture and place on the appropriate season

Summer

Autumn

Winter

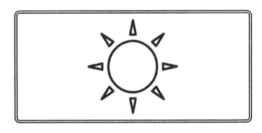

Spring

Months of the Season

Cut around and paste the months into the correct season

Summer

Autumn

Winter

Spring

March
April
May

December
January
February

September
October
November

June
July
August

SCHOOL OBJECTS

GLI OGGETTI SCOLASTICI

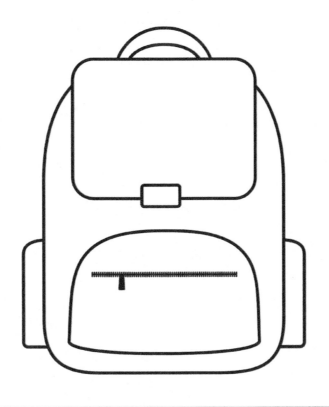

What's in my school bag?

Write or draw all the items you need to pack in your school bag every day.

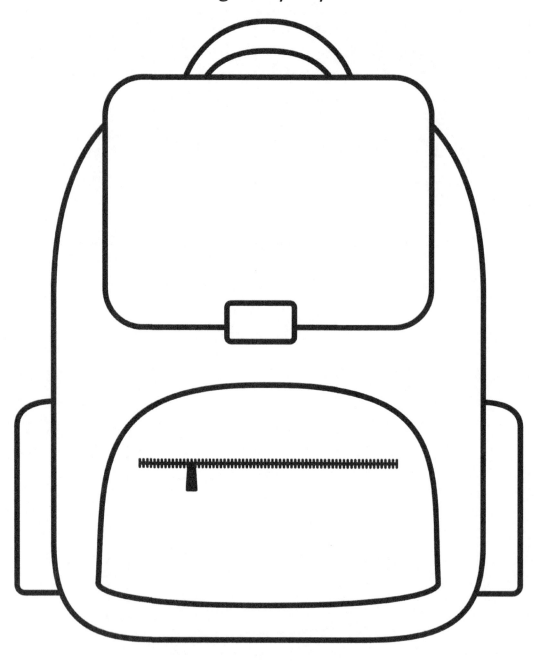

school supplies

Match the words with the pictures.

pen   bag   paper   sharpener   ruler   book   clip
notebook   stapler   eraser   scissors   glue

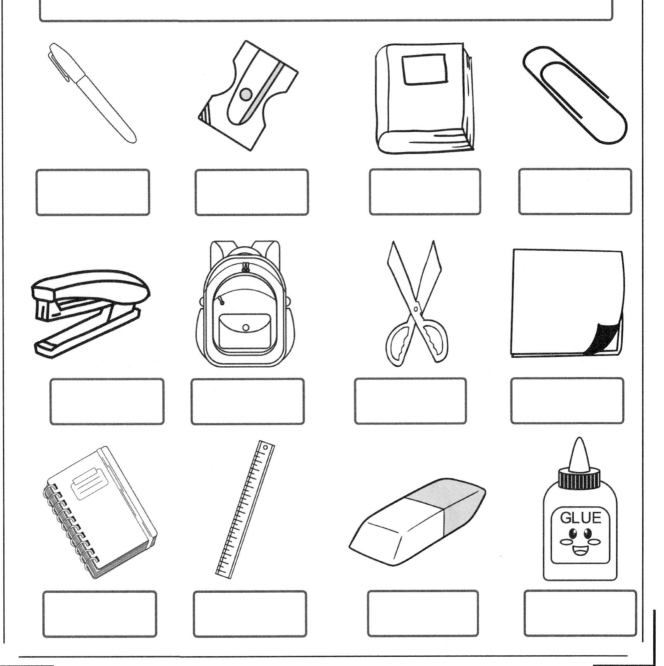

Write your answers on the black beside each picture

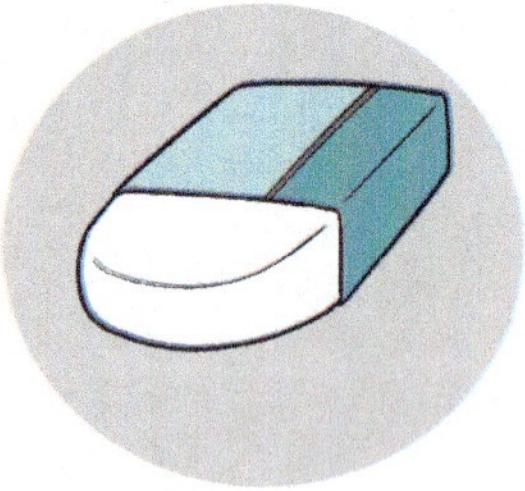

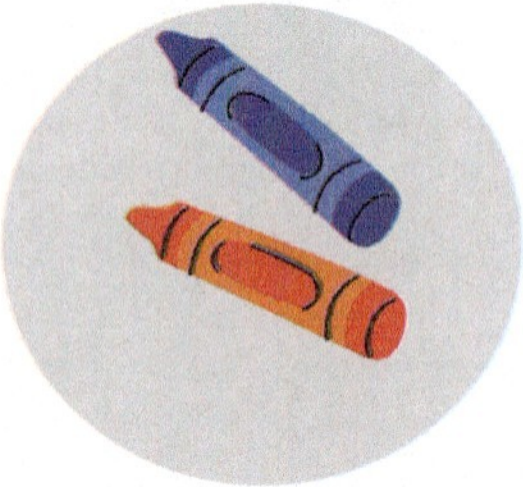

_____

_____

_____

_____

_____

Write your answers on the black beside each picture

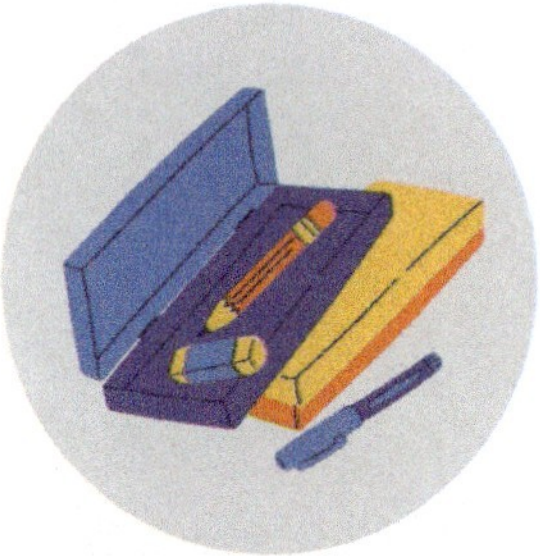

_____

_____

_____

_____

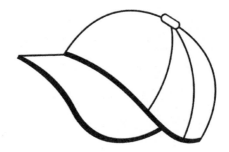

CLOTHES

I VESTITI

Clothes

Match the words with the pictures.

| dress | t-shirt | tie | sunglasses | cap | pants |
| socks | boots | belt | jacket | shoes | shorts |

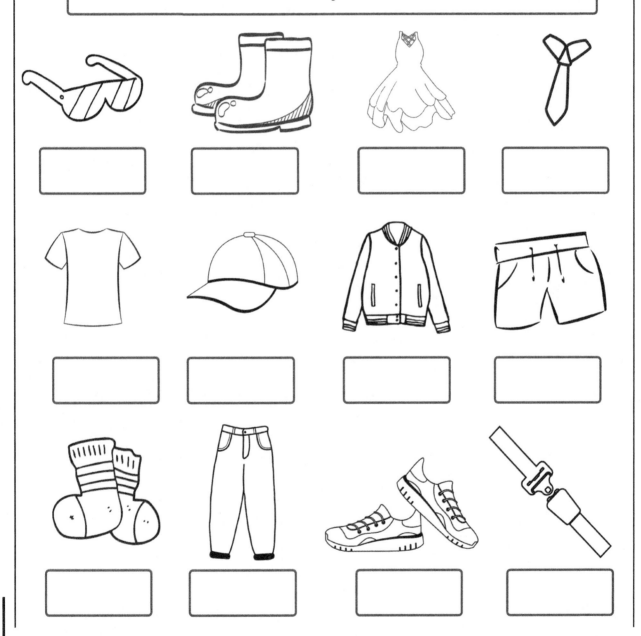

Color the clothes based on the weather

warm - yellow   cold - blue

Word Search

Can you find the words hidden in the puzzle?

```
V S D S S O B T N T F K
H L L H U S A N D A L S
O A I O S L T E B P I T
T A T R V K H R C A P T
N M N T Y L I A T A F E
D R E S S A N R L E L T
A T A G P D G D T L O R
S U N G L A S S E S P U
S E N G H N U S E S S N
S A N G L B I K I N I K
O T S H I R T D F O S S
A T O H F R V S O M E T
```

- CAP
- SKIRT
- BIKINI
- HAT
- TRUNKS
- SHORTS
- T-SHIRT
- FLIP-FLOPS
- BATHING SUIT
- SUNGLASSES
- SANDALS
- DRESS

WEATHER

IL TEMPO ATMOSFERICO

THE WEATHER

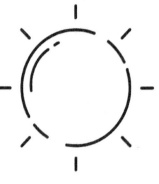  

IT'S SUNNY   IT'S CLOUDY   IT'S RAINY

IT'S SNOWY   IT'S WINDY   IT'S STORMY

IT'S HOT   IT'S COLD

Food and drink

CIBO E BEVANDE

apple	banana	strawberry
		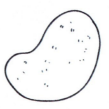
corn	carrot	potato

bread	fries	Icecreme

hamburger

jam

rice   egg   cheese

Orange juice   coke

FOOD

3 LETTER WORDS

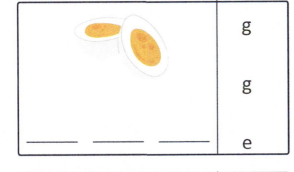

g
g
e
___ ___ ___

e
p
i
___ ___ ___

m
j
a
___ ___ ___

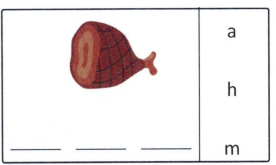

a
h
m
___ ___ ___

4 LETTER WORDS

k
a
e
c
___ ___ ___ ___

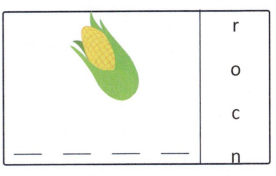

r
o
c
n
___ ___ ___ ___

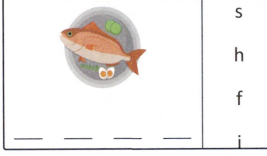

s
h
f
i
___ ___ ___ ___

r
p
a
e
___ ___ ___ ___

TOYS

I GIOCATTOLI

Children's Toys

Boat	Bicycle	Ball
Bird	Car	Doll
Rope	Plane	Dinosaur
Piano	Telephone	Bear

Children's Toys

Duck	Unicorn	Truck

Skate Board	Top	Play House

Star	Rocket	Xylophone

Stroller	Robot	Rock Horse

Trace and write

duck - drum - doll - maracas

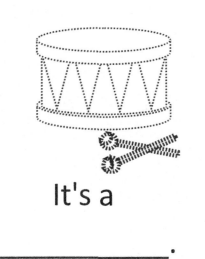

It's a

_____.

They're

_____.

It's a

_____.

It's a

_____.

Trace and write

ball - yo-yo - kite - rocket

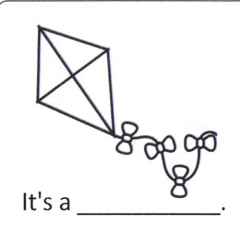

It's a _____.

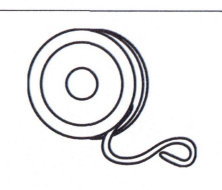

It's a _____.

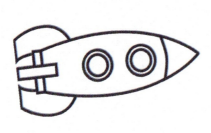

It's a _____.

It's a _____.

Body Parts

Mouth   Teeth   Chin

Eyebrows   Eyes   Arm

Nose   Neck   Tongue

Ear   Elbow   Hand

Hair   Belly Button   Foot

PARTS OF THE BODY

Label the body parts in this diagram.

chest   foot   hand   eyebrow   eye

stomach   hair   mouth   ear   shoulder

PARTS OF THE BODY

Label the body parts in this diagram.

chest   foot   hand   eyebrow   eye

stomach   hair   mouth   ear   shoulder

FEELS

LE EMOZIONI

Today I feel...

Circle the way you feel.

Happy   Sad   Angry

Nervous   Excited   Tired

Worried   Focused   Confused   Joyful

Confident   Upset

Today I am... _____

Draw a face showing the way you feel today..

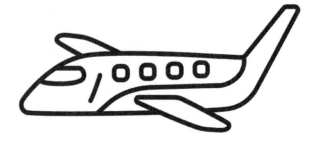

MEANS OF TRANSPORT

Transport

Colour the means of transport according to where they go.

Transport

Label the means of transport

bike - underground – bus - lorry - rocket - boat
ship - car - helicopter - scooter - plane - skateboard

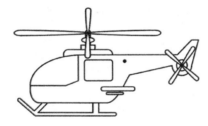

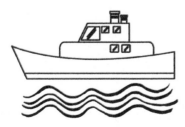

FAMILY MEMBERS

Family Members Word Search

S	Y	F	A	T	H	E	R	T	U	R	Q
M	O	E	E	A	D	O	A	U	N	T	A
S	R	N	C	M	D	A	A	N	C	R	G
F	P	C	C	O	D	O	C	C	L	R	R
G	T	A	B	T	U	O	H	L	E	N	A
R	H	D	R	H	I	S	T	E	R	N	N
A	E	E	O	E	N	V	I	S	E	N	D
N	R	N	T	R	N	I	X	N	T	R	M
D	V	T	H	A	D	T	C	C	H	R	A
P	P	I	E	O	S	I	S	T	E	R	V
A	V	S	R	A	D	Z	C	G	R	R	E
S	D	A	U	G	H	T	E	R	O	H	T

SON FATHER COUSIN GRANDPA

AUNT MOTHER BROTHER GRANDMA

UNCLE SISTER PARENTS DAUGHTER

PRESENT AND PAST FAMILY LIFE

Complete your family tree below

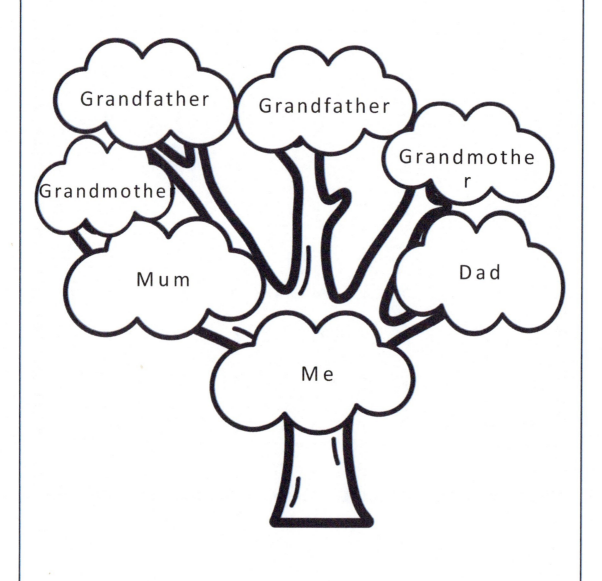

Daily routine

Daily Routine

Directions: Answer the questions below.

1. What time do you wake up?
_____

2. What time do you eat breakfast?
_____

3. What time do you go to school?
_____

4. What time do you eat lunch?
_____

5. What time do you sleep at night?
_____

Animals A to Z

Color the animaL

ALLIGATOR   BEAR   CAT

DOG   ELEPHANT   FISH

HIPPO   IGUANA   GOAT

Animals A to Z

Color the animaL

JELLYFISH   KOALA   LION

MONKEY   NARWHAT   OCTOPUS

PANDA   QUAIL   RACCOON

Animals A to Z

Color the animaL

SNAKE	TURTLE	URCHIN

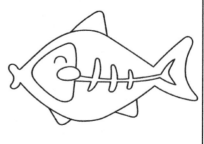

YAK	ZEBRA	X-RAY FISCH

VAMPIRE BAT	WHALE

Farm Animals

Trace the names of the animals and color them.

duck

dog

cat

cow

rabbit

horse

sheep

Jungle Animals

Trace the names of the animals and colour them.

lion　giraffe　monkey　parrot

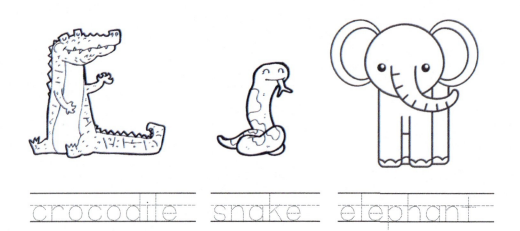

crocodile　snake　elephant

OPPOSITES

Opposites

Trace and colour the correct picture.

OPPOSITES
Cut and match.

ADJECTIVES

ADJECTIVES

View the picture on the right, then use an adjective (describing word) to fill in the blank space, best describing the picture.

The cat has _____ orange hair.	
The cactus has _____ sharp spikes.	
The soup was _____ and tasty.	
The fish is _____ and large.	

Adjectives

Read and circle.

A long train

An old phone

A big dog

An ugly monster

A new bag

A short monster

A small ball

DEGREES OF ADJECTIVES

Complete each set by writing the appropriate degrees of comparison.

big   _____   biggest

_____   longer   longest

  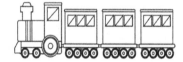

_____   faster   fastest

small   _____   smallest

What's time is it?

WHAT TIME IS IT?

Draw the hour hand and the minute hand of the clock according to the time written below

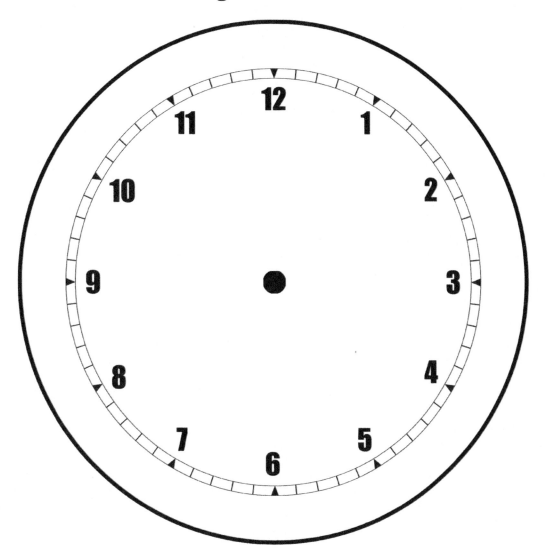

IT'S TEN.

WHAT TIME IS IT?

Draw the hour hand and the minute hand of the clock according to the time written below

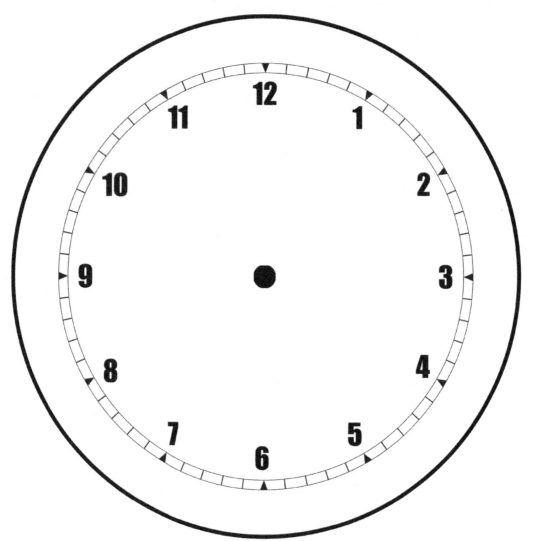

IT'S HALF PAST NINE.

WHAT TIME IS IT?

Draw the hour hand and the minute hand of the clock according to the time written below

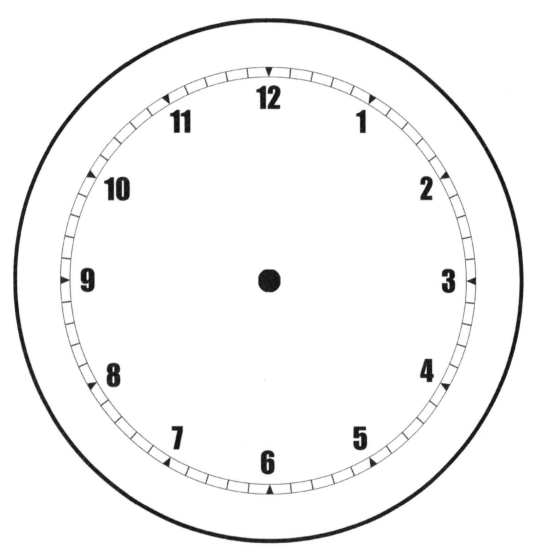

IT'S HALF PAST NINE.

WHAT TIME IS IT?

Draw the hour hand and the minute hand of the clock according to the time written below

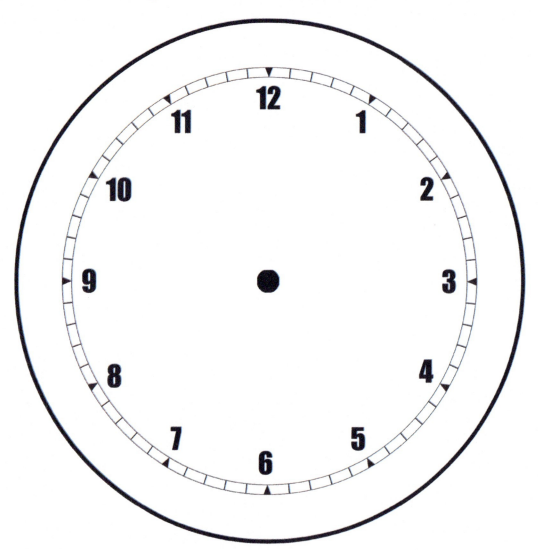

IT'S QUARTER TO THREE.

WHAT TIME IS IT?

Draw the hour hand and the minute hand of the clock according to the time written below

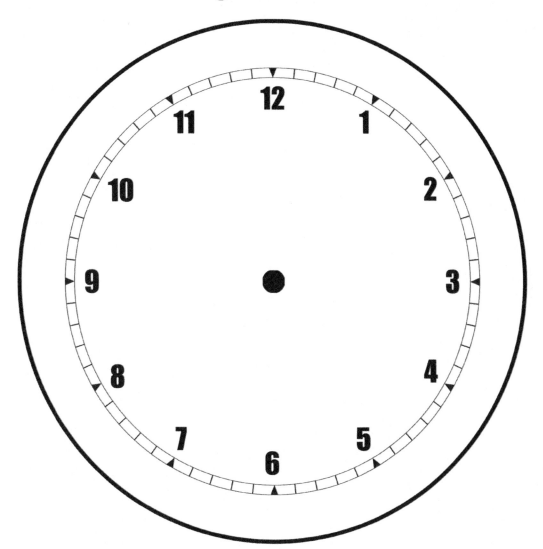

IT'S QUARTER PAST SIX.

TIME: HALF PAST

Write the time on the clocks below:

1:30   12:30   9:30

2:30   6:30   10:30

7:30   11:30

Add the hour of coloring to the clock's

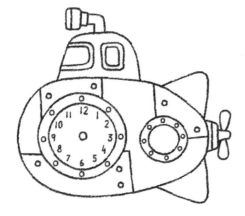

WHAT'S TIME IS IT?

....
....

WHAT'S TIME IS IT?

....
....

WHAT'S TIME IS IT?

....
....

I Can

What can you do? Complete the sentences with can or can't.

Can / Can't

Anna **can** ride her bike

Emma **can't** ride her bike

1- I _____ ride a bike.

2- I _____ swim.

3- I _____ play football

4- I _____ rollerskate.

5- I _____ do gymnastics.

6- I _____ dance.

7- I _____ play basketball.

Can you do it?

Directions: Read the questions and circle your answer.

Can you ride a bicycle?

Yes, I can.   No, I can't.

Can you climb a tree?

Yes, I can.   No, I can't.

Can you swim?

Yes, I can.   No, I can't.

Can you sing a song?

Yes, I can.   No, I can't.

Can you dance?

Yes, I can.   No, I can't.

Action Words

Circle the correct picture mentioned in the sentence.

I can read.	
I can jump.	
I can sing.	
I can climb.	
I can clap.	

Read the story and answer the following questions.

Tim The Kid

Tim is a kid.

He is six.

Tim saw a wig in a bin.

He wore the funny wig.

Tim got his bag with a zip.

He went home with his wig.

Tim is a _____.   kid   adult

Tim saw a _____ in a bin.   bib   wig

Tim got his bag with a _____.   zip   pin

Read the story and answer the following questions.

Jim's Pig

Jim got a pink pig.

His name is Kit.

Jim and Kit went to eat a big fig.

Kit, the pig, likes Jim.

Kit is a happy pink pig.

Jim got a pink _____.

cow   pig

Jim and Kit went to eat a big _____.

fig   kiwi

Kit is a _____ pink pig.

happy   sad

Read the story and answer the following questions.

Zen The Hen

This is Zen.

She is a hen.

Zen likes to be fed.

She begs for ten red apples.

The men gets ten red apples.

Zen the hen went back to her den.

Zen is a _____.

She begs for ten red _____.

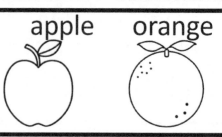

Zen the hen went back to her _____.

Have got

Have you got...?

Read and answer the questions.

	Hair	Eyes
Anna	brown	green
Amy	black	black
Billy	blond	blue

1- Have you got blonde hair, Anna?
_____

2- Have you got green eyes, Billy?
_____

3- Have you got blue eyes, Amy?
_____

4- Have you got black hair, Anna?
_____

What do you have in your toy box?

1- I have got a ....

2- I have got a ....

3- I have got a ....

4- I have got a ....

5- I have got a ....

6- I have got a ....

7- I have got a ....

8- I have got ....

Lunchtime

Complete the sentences with food words bellow.

Chicken- carrots- cakes- steak- sandwich- peas- banana- apple- chips- pizza- sausages

I have got _____, _____ and _____.

I have got an _____, cheese _____ and a _____.

I have got _____ and _____.

I have got _____, _____ and _____.

Verb to be

VERB TO BE

Complete the sentences with the correct answer.

1. The dog _____ in front of the house.
2. They _____ playing football outside,
3. I _____ in Primary 4.
4. She _____ my grandmother.
5. You _____ are my friend,

Create your own sentences.

1. _____

2. _____

3. _____

4. _____

5. _____

There is/ There are

Use there is or there are

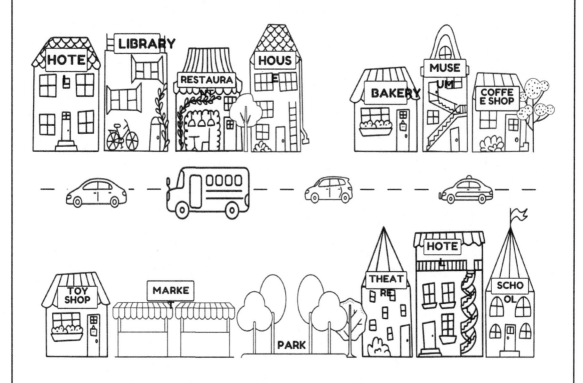

1. .... a theatre..
2. .... cars..
3. .... trees.
4. .... a school
5. .... two hotels.
6. .... a park.
7. .... a bakery.
8. .... a bus.

Prepositions of place

PREPOSITIONS OF place

1- The cat is on the sofa.   T or F
2- There is a dog in front of the door.   T or F
3- The plant is between the sofa and the door.   T or F
4- There are two paintings on the wall.   T or F
5- The mirror is near the lampshade.   T or F
6- The rug is in front of the sofa.   T or F
7- There are books on the shelf.   T or F
8- The vase is next to the lamp.   T or F
9- The window is behind the plant.   T or F
10- There pillows are under the sofa.   T or F

PREPOSITIONS

Fill in the blanks using the following list of prepositions:

The bear is standing _____ the stool.

The sun is shining _____ the tree.

The rocking horse is _____ the table.

The cat is _____ the treasure chest.

The flowers are _____ the vase.

The bee is buzzing _____ the flowers.

The table is _____ the vase.

The stool is _____ the bear.

above

in

below

under

above

under

on

inside

Possessive pronous

Possessive Pronouns

Circle the possessive pronouns in the sentences.

- I will show you to your room. Ours is next door.
- This lunch box is mine. It has my name on it.
- Those gifts are Jake's, and over there are yours.
- His ball is big, but mine is small.
- I bought these toys for you. These are yours.
- That truck belongs to Uncle Tom. It is his.
- Michelle wanted the medal to be hers.
- Our team beat theirs in the football match.
- The pink bicycle is mine.
- It's ours. We bought it at the mall.
- I saw your phone on the desk. I think it is yours.
- Ana left her bag. These colored pencils are hers.
- This is my grandpa's shirt. This is his.
- I am sure those glasses are mine.
- My friends played this morning. That ball is theirs.

WHAT'S THE PRONOUN?

Fill in the blanks to complete the sentences.

- Matthew has a blue car. That blue car is _____.

- My husband and I bought this house. It is _____.

- I made a sandwich. It is _____.

- The black laptop is _____. My dad bought it for me.

- My sister left it. These keys are _____.

- Geno and Gel made a project. Next to the blue desk are _____.

- This pencil case is _____. You left it.

- That blue ruler is _____. It has my name on it.

- The jeans are _____. She bought those yesterday.

- My cousins and I made this toy. It is _____.

Choose the correct possessive pronoun inside the box.

hers   his   mine   its

theirs   ours   yours

This is my pet.
This is _____ bone.

This is Oliver.
These shoes are _____.

My name is Ana.
This doll is _____.

This is my family.
This house is _____.

These are my friends.
These balls are _____.

This is my mom.
These clothes are _____.

WRITE IT!

Write a sentence for each picture.

_____

_____

_____

_____

WHAT'S THE PRONOUN?

Replace the personal pronouns with possessive pronouns.

This skateboard is (you).

_____

There is a squirrel in the tree. These nuts are (it).

_____

The bracelet is (she).

_____

These candies are (they).

_____

This luggage belongs to me. It is (my).

_____

Some-Any

SOME OR ANY

Fill in the blanks with the correct answer.

- We need _____ tomatoes for lunch.
- The teacher gave _____ worksheet to the students.
- They don't have _____ books at the library.
- Judy doesn't have _____ glue.
- My aunt always puts _____ sugar in her coffee.
- Does the teacher have _____ marker?
- There are _____ beautiful places here.
- I want to buy _____ new books.
- Do you have _____ brothers or sisters?
- Can I have _____ water?
- There isn't _____ cheese left.
- Do you have _____ pins?
- My grandmother needs _____ bread for sandwiches.
- I'd like to eat _____ chocolate.
- Does she have _____ pen?

READ AND IDENTIFY

Fill in the blanks with the correct answer.

- Mom bought new _____ (appliance / appliances) for our new house.
- I like to eat _____ (cheese / cheeses).
- My grandpa likes to drink _____ (coffee / coffees) every morning.
- Bettany is my new _____ (friends / friend) at school.
- The bookstore sells _____ famous (book / books).
- (Sugars / Sugar) _____ is sweet.
- There are ten _____ (desks / desk) in the classroom.
- My cousin has brown _____ (hair / hairs).
- I brought an _____ (umbrella / umbrellas).
- Do you have any _____ (pet / pets)?

CLIL

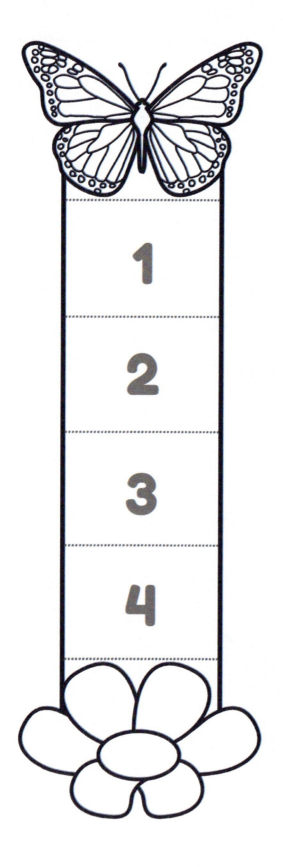

Life Cycle of a BUTTERFLY

Instructions:
- Color the butterfly and the stages of its life cycle.
- Cut and paste the pictures in order on the boxes.
- Cut around the butterfly template and fold the dotted horizontal lines into pleats.

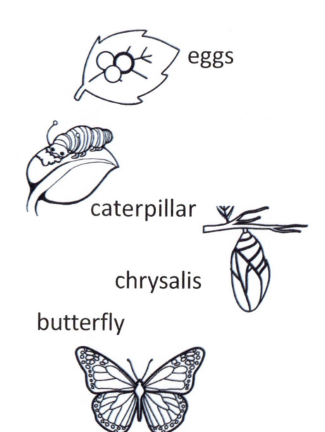

eggs

caterpillar

chrysalis

butterfly

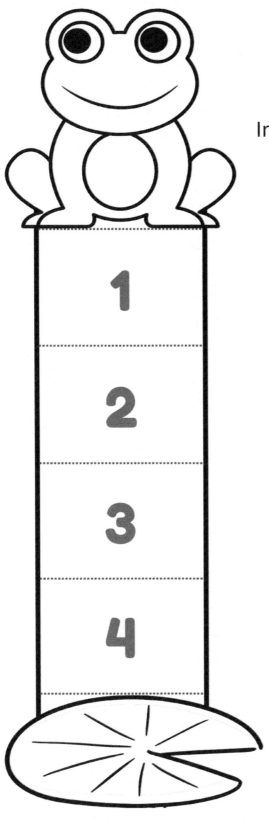

Life Cycle of a
FROG

Instructions:
- Color the frog and the stages of its life cycle.
- Cut and paste the pictures in order on the boxes.
- Cut around the frog template and fold the dotted horizontal lines into pleats.

eggs

tadpole

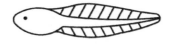

froglet

frog

PARTS OF A PLANT

Cut out the words in the boxes below, then use paste the words in the boxes.

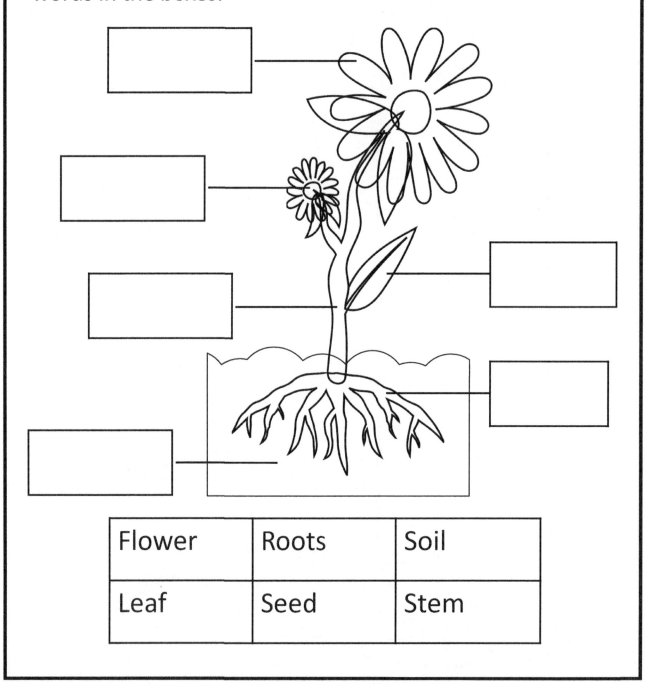

Flower	Roots	Soil
Leaf	Seed	Stem

ACTIVITY BOOK

XMAS

HALLOWEEN

EART DAY

ST PATRICK

GRANDPARENT'S DAY

EASTER

MOTHER'S DAY

DAD'S DAY

Happy St Patrick's Day

ST PATRICK'S DAY
WORD SEARCH

P	A	T	R	I	C	K	O	N	U	M
W	D	R	R	T	N	I	A	S	A	I
I	E	S	E	T	H	N	G	R	C	R
N	T	C	E	L	O	L	C	E	L	E
W	L	U	C	K	A	H	G	R	O	L
O	R	O	H	R	E	N	T	E	V	A
B	P	O	T	A	G	E	D	M	E	N
N	E	L	D	L	O	G	E	M	R	D
I	L	H	T	S	E	I	R	P	I	S
A	N	E	E	R	G	I	T	S	R	F
R	S	H	A	M	R	O	C	K	B	O

MARCH   IRELAND   SAINT   LUCK

PRIEST   RAINBOW   PATRICK   GREEN

CLOVER   GOLD   SHAMROCK   POT

All About Mum

My mum's name is _____

My mum is _____ years old

Her favourite colour is _____

Her favourite food is _____

My mum is really good at _____

My favourite thing about my mum is _____

MOTHER'S DAY
WORD SEARCH

N	A	T	E	L	T	N	E	G	U	G
U	D	R	D	E	T	O	V	E	D	R
R	E	T	E	T	M	N	G	C	C	A
T	T	R	E	V	O	L	C	R	L	N
U	D	O	C	K	T	H	G	I	O	D
R	E	F	H	R	H	U	G	S	E	M
E	D	M	T	A	E	E	D	M	R	O
N	L	O	D	L	R	G	E	M	A	T
I	I	C	T	S	E	I	R	R	C	H
A	H	L	A	I	C	E	P	S	A	E
R	C	P	R	O	T	E	C	T	S	R

MOTHER   NURTURE   CHILD   HUGS

SPECIAL   CARE   GRANDMOTHER   PROTECTS

LOVE   COMFORT   GENTLE   DEVOTED

All About
DAD!

Dad and me!

My dad's name is
_____.
He is _____.
He does _____ at work. My dad's favorite thing to do on the weekend is
_____.
My dad is always saying, "_____".
I know how much dad loves me when he
_____.
My favorite thing to do with dad is _____.
I love dad more than _____.
Love,
_____

Happy Grandparent's Day

I wanted to show you how much I care.

I call my Grandmother_____

We have so much fun when we_____

My Grandma cooks the best _____

The thing I love most about my grandma is
_____
_____

Here is a picture of the two of us.

I love you! Love,_____

Merry Christmas

Find-a-word
CHRISTMAS

P	U	C	B	R	E	L	M	T	E	J
C	H	R	I	S	T	M	A	S	S	O
B	O	R	R	C	R	S	N	S	D	S
U	H	A	T	V	E	A	G	E	R	E
N	S	D	H	O	E	V	E	T	E	P
A	N	G	E	L	S	I	R	A	H	H
R	O	L	Y	A	S	O	R	M	P	N
B	L	E	S	S	U	U	G	S	E	D
B	O	R	N	E	S	R	T	U	H	E
B	E	T	H	L	E	H	E	M	S	F
S	O	N	A	R	J	E	Y	R	A	M

Christmas is celebrated annually on the 25th of December. On this day, Christians celebrate the **birth** of **Jesus**, God's **son**, in Bethlehem. Jesus was born to parents **Mary** and **Joseph**, who returned to **Bethlehem** under an order for all people to return to their home towns so they could be taxed. There was no room at any of the inns, so Mary gave birth to Jesus in a **manger**. **Angels** appears to **shepherds** in the field, singing praises that the **Saviour** had been **born**.

CHRISTMAS CARDS

There's snow one just like you!

Merry Christmas!

Love,_____

You are the coolest person I SNOW!

Merry Christmas!

Love,_____

Happy Halloween

I am going to dress up as:

_____

Halloween Word Search

```
P U M P K I N L T
C A N D Y U P I R
W D R A C U L A I
I A S T R E A T C
T N W N Y D E S K
C O S T U M E C E
H Z O M B I E A N
K U S N O C T R D
P I G H O S T Y W
```

treat   scary   candy   party
trick   boo   zombie   witch
ghost   dracula   costume   pumpkin

Count and Circle

149

Happy Easter

Color the picture by following the instructions.

- Color the bunny gray.
- Color the bunny's ears pink.
- Color the carrots orange.
- Color the first egg pink and yellow.
- Color the second egg purple and orange.
- Color the third egg blue and green.
- Color the fourth egg green and pink.
- Draw a sun and a cloud.

BACK TO SCHOOL
WORD SEARCH

R	E	C	E	S	S	K	O	N	L	M
W	M	A	T	H	S	I	A	S	E	I
S	P	E	L	L	I	N	G	R	A	R
N	T	C	E	S	S	A	L	C	R	E
R	L	U	C	K	D	H	G	R	N	L
E	R	O	H	L	U	N	C	H	V	A
H	P	L	A	Y	S	E	E	M	E	N
C	E	L	D	K	O	G	E	I	R	D
A	L	H	O	S	E	I	R	P	R	S
E	N	O	E	R	E	T	I	R	W	F
T	B	H	A	M	L	O	O	H	C	S

SCHOOL	CLASS	PLAY	SPELLING
FRIENDS	LUNCH	LEARN	WRITE
TEACHER	RECESS	MATHS	BOOKS

Printed by Amazon Italia Logistica S.r.l.
Torrazza Piemonte (TO), Italy